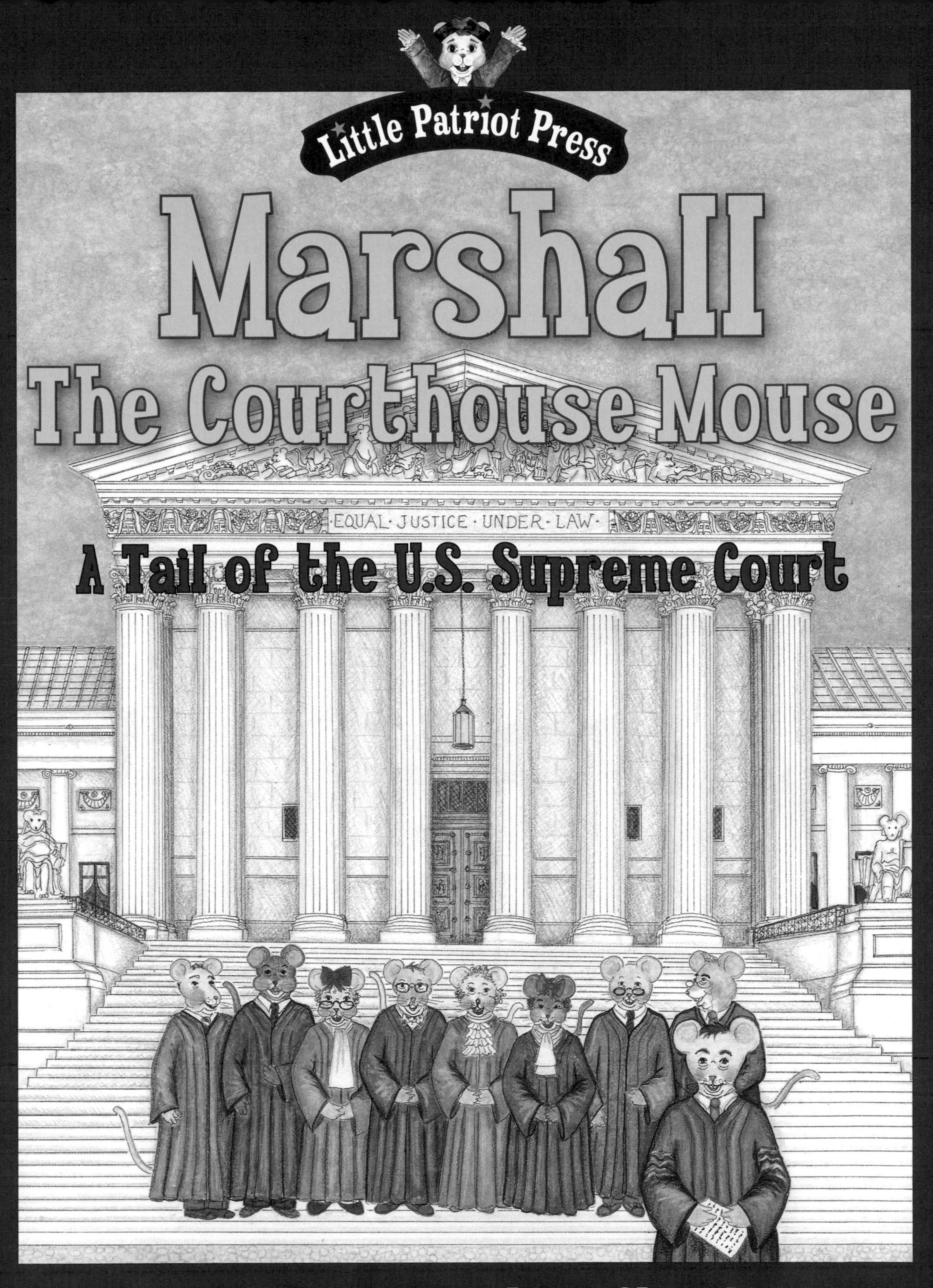

By Peter W. Barnes and Cheryl Shaw Barnes

Cataloging-in-Publication data on file with the Library of Congress
ISBN 978-1-59698-789-0

Published in the United States by
Little Patriot Press
an imprint of Regnery Publishing, Inc.
One Massachusetts Avenue, NW
Washington, DC 20001
www.Regnery.com

Manufactured in the United States of America
10 9 8 7 6 5 4 3 2 1

Books are available in quantity for promotional or premium use. For information on discounts and terms write to Director of Special Sales, Regnery Publishing, Inc., One Massachusetts Avenue, NW, Washington, DC, 20001, or call 202-216-0600.

Distributed to the trade by
Perseus Distribution
387 Park Avenue South
New York, NY 10016

We dedicate this book

to James Stafford (1906–1990), grandfather,
judge, country lawyer, and poet.

—P.W.B. and C.S.B.

*"The time has come when I must give up the farm ...
I am too old to do the fixin'."*

Turtles found in sculpture in various locations around the Supreme Court building suggest the slow and steady path of justice. Look for a turtle hidden in every illustration in this book!

Hear ye, hear ye! All rise and draw near!
America's mice, with good will and good cheer,

Are pleased to announce and proud to report,
The opening term of the Mouse Supreme Court!

The court now in session is nine special mice—
They're all very smart and they're all very nice!
They are called "justices," and their great contribution
Is to guard and protect the Mouse Constitution!

The one in the middle, with the bars on his sleeve,
Is the *Chief* Justice—Marshall J. Mouse, we believe.
All justices are equal, but he is the one
Who makes sure the work of the court all gets done.

This court—the "High Court"—is the one most renowned.
But there are other courts, too, if you just look around.
There are courts in each city and county and town.
(The mice even have a few courts underground!)

In all of these courts, a judge is in charge.
Who sits at a "bench"—a desk very large.
But "lawyers" and "juries" can also be there,
To help judges make every court just and fair.

Our laws are the rules that all must obey,
To be a good person—or mouse—every day.
The law says be careful when riding your bike,
So you don't end up hitting somebody you like.

Another law says that it's not right to steal
A book, piece of candy, or automobile!
And laws say that everyone must go to school—
Don't you agree that's a wonderful rule?

But one group of laws stands above all the others,
Declared long ago by our nation's forefathers,
Who wrote down on paper, through long days and nights,
Our grand Constitution and great Bill of Rights.

These documents gave us (you really should read 'em)
A promise to all of liberty and freedom.
They gave everybody the freedom to vote,
The freedom to worship, and also, please note:

The right to free speech, and the right to decide
How to live your own life—how to live it with pride.
These rights are so special, we all must respect them!
The Supreme Court's job is to preserve and protect them.

Sunday

Cheddar

Monday

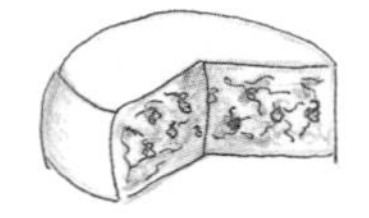

Roquefort

Tuesday

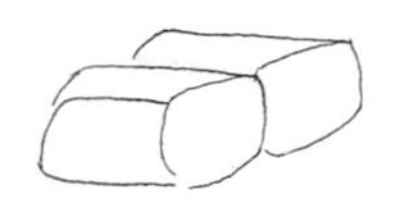

Mozzarella

Wednesday

Swiss Cheese

Thursday

Parmesan

Friday

American

Saturday

Philadelphia Cream

It does this whenever it chooses to hear
A question or "case" of a law that's unclear.
For disputes about laws aren't all that unusual—
In fact, some laws can be "*un*-Constitutional"!

Here's an example the Mouse Congress created:
It once passed a law that directed and stated
That mice could not eat the same cheese every day—
It was a strict law all mice had to obey!

It said that on Sundays, they had to eat Cheddar;
On Mondays was Roquefort, which many liked better.
On Tuesdays, everyone ate Mozzarella,
From the smallest mouse girl to the biggest mouse fella.

Each Wednesday, Swiss cheese was on every plate.
On Thursdays, Parmesan everyone ate.
On Fridays, American cheese was supreme.
And Saturdays, just Philadelphia Cream.

But some of the mice had thought all along,
"This law is confusing and odd—and just wrong!
Each mouse family should always be able
To put any cheese that it wants on its table!"

But other mice liked the rules, thinking them good—
They wanted the cheese law to stay as it stood.
So one side against it, one side in support—
Who decides? Why, of course—the Mouse Supreme Court!

CITIZEN MICE FOR REPEAL OF CHEESE LAWS
MICE CITIZENS FOR UPHOLDING CHEESE LAWS
MOUSE CITIZENS FOR CHEESE CHOICE
MICE AGAINST CHEESE CHANGE
CHEESE CHOICE
KEEP SWISS ON WEDNESDAYS
CHEESE CHOICE
NO CHEESE CHANGE
OICE OF HEESES NYTIME NYDAY
AGAINST CHEESE CHANGE
CHEESE DAYS LIKE THE OLD DAYS

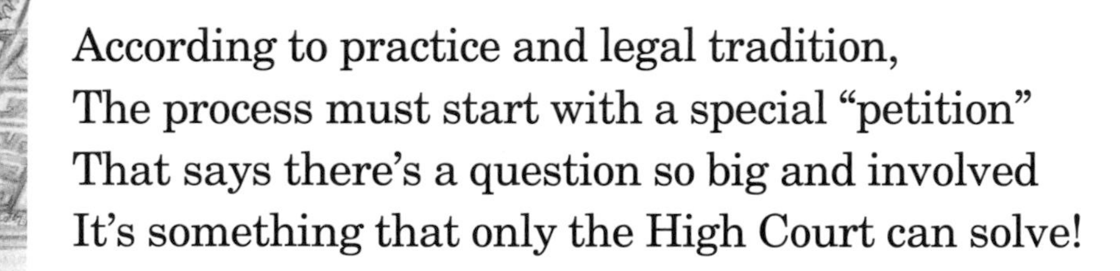

According to practice and legal tradition,
The process must start with a special “petition”
That says there’s a question so big and involved
It’s something that only the High Court can solve!

In this case, the justices had to address
This difficult question, which went, more or less:
“Does the cheese law deny any mice, large or small,
Their *Constitutional rights*—any at all?”

To make a decision, the justices start
With “oral arguments,” from lawyers quite smart.
Each lawyer discusses one point of view—
The justices listen, and ask questions, too.

But justices need more than that to decide.
So they have special helpers, called "clerks," who provide
Extra research and work, and at the start of each fall,
The Chief Justice meets with the clerks, one and all.

"I'm sure you all know," the Chief Justice said,
"How important your work is, how much is ahead.
But the work may not be as hard as it looks—
To help in each case, you should all hit the books!"

So off to the library they run in a dash,
Then into the bookshelves they fly like a flash!
There are clerks at each desk, there are clerks in each chair.
There are books piled up—books and clerks everywhere!

This work can take weeks—sometimes it takes months,
While the justices study and meet more than once
In private, "in conference," to talk and review,
To decide on each case, what's the best thing to do.

In the cheese case, Marshall stood up from the table.
"Fellow justices," he said, "I am sure you are able
To see that this case has a simple solution,
For it's plain and it's clear from our great Constitution,

"That its words and its meaning grant a most basic right,
That allows any mouse with a good appetite
To choose the cheese he or she *wants* for a meal—
Swiss, Bleu, or Cheddar—whatever they feel!

"This means that the cheese law, I'm sure you can see
Must be *struck down* now—Constitutionally!"
"Hear, hear!" said the others. "We consent and agree!"
And they voted with Marshall, unani-mouse-ly!

To give their decision, the justices next
Wrote down an "opinion," their words put in text.
And by court tradition, what they had agreed
Was printed on paper for all mice to read.

Cite as: 522 U.S. 345 (2012)

Opinion of the Court

NOTICE: This opinion is subject to formal revision before publication in the preliminary print of the United States Reports. Readers are requested to notify the Reporter of Decisions, Supreme Court of the United Mice, Washington, D.C. 20543, of any typographical or other formal errors, in order that corrections may be made before the preliminary print goes to press.

SUPREME COURT OF THE UNITED MICE

No. 98-123

FREEDOM OF CHEESE COALITION, ET AL., PETITIONERS *v.* DAILY CHEESE GROUP ET AL.

ON WRIT OF CERTIORARI TO THE UNITED STATES COURT OF APPEALS FOR THE ELEVENTH CIRCUIT

[May 18, 2012]

CHIEF JUSTICE MARSHALL delivered the opinion of the court.

We granted certiorari in this case to determine whether the Daily Cheese Act of 2011 violated the liberty interests of mice by denying them the freedom to eat any cheese they want on any day of the week. We hold that the law does violate such liberties. We conclude that the District Court in this case erred in its finding that the law did not run counter to the collective provisions of the Bill of Rights and the Constitution.

I

Petitioner William G. Washingtail, chairman of the Freedom of Cheese Coalition, was arrested by cheese police in June 2011 for eating cheddar cheese at his home on a Wednesday, when the Daily Cheese Act required all mice to eat Swiss cheese on that day. Petitioner declared his dining action a protest against unfair restriction on his right to eat whatever

EQUAL · JUSTICE · UNDER · LAW ·

The justices also "hand down" their decision,
Announced from their bench with care and precision,
Read aloud by a justice, a great declaration,
To all who are gathered and the rest of the nation.

In this way, their decision is spread far and wide—
It proclaims the new rules by which all must abide.
Each decision makes sure that we all understand
That our great Constitution is the law of the land!

And that night, at the tables of mice everywhere
There were all kinds of cheeses to enjoy and to share.
Thanks to nine justices, who care and support
And protect all our rights at the great Supreme Court!

The Tail End

Resources for Parents and Teachers

★ ★ ★

The main character of the story, Marshall, is named after John Marshall (1755–1835), the Supreme Court's Chief Justice from 1801 to 1835. Through his strong leadership, Marshall helped establish the court as a truly co-equal branch of government with the president and the Congress. In 1803, Marshall wrote a landmark decision, *Marbury v. Madison*, striking down an act of Congress that was in conflict with the Constitution. With this decision, Marshall and the court created the concept of "judicial review," which established the Supreme Court's power to declare laws unconstitutional. There are several portraits of Marshall in the building, and a statue of him sits in the Lower Great Hall.

Marshall is also the last name of another pioneering justice, Thurgood Marshall (1908–1993), the first African-American appointed to the Court. Before he became an associate justice in 1967, Marshall served as the chief lawyer for the National Association for the Advancement of Colored Persons (NAACP). He presented the argument before the Court that resulted in the 1954 decision *Brown v. Board of Education*, which declared that racial segregation in public schools was unconstitutional.

The Supreme Court of the United States was created by America's Founding Fathers in the Constitution of 1787. But while the chief executive worked at the White House and Congress worked in the Capitol, the Court did not have a home of its own until 1935. Before then, it worked for about a decade from buildings in Philadelphia, and next, for 135 years, out of chambers in the Capitol.

It was a former president who became Chief Justice, William Howard Taft, who spearheaded the campaign in the

The Tail End

Resources for Parents and Teachers

1920s to construct a separate building for the Court. After he convinced Congress to approve the structure, lawmakers created the Supreme Court Building Commission in 1928. The commission hired a prominent architect of the time, Cass Gilbert, to design the building. He chose a neo-classical style for the marble building that drew upon the classic structures of ancient Greece and Rome for inspiration—grand columns, broad flights of steps, bronze doors, magnificent plazas, and beautiful friezes (sculptured scenes on stone). The building was completed in April 1935.

In this book, illustrator Cheryl Shaw Barnes also reproduced the architecture of other types of courthouses. She has included the simple brick colonial design of the courthouse in her hometown of Alexandria, Virginia, across the Potomac River from Washington, as well as the Berrien County courthouse in Berrien Springs, Michigan, which was built in 1839 and is a classic Greek revival structure.

In illustrations for the Supreme Court of the U.S., Cheryl Barnes chose to highlight several of the more famous rooms of the building. The main public room, the **Courtroom**, is in the heart of the structure, where justices meet to hear oral arguments of cases, to announce opinions, and transact the court's other public business. The room is nearly square, with columns 30 feet tall and the ceiling 44 feet overhead. The walls of the upper third of the room are a marble frieze by the sculptor Adolph A. Weinman; it depicts historical lawgivers, such as Moses, Hammurabi, and John Marshall, and allegorical figures such as *Justice*.

The **West Conference Room** is paneled with white oak. The East and West Conference Rooms are used for a variety of functions, including

The Tail End
Resources for Parents and Teachers

events with large audiences, receptions, dinners, and annual reunions some justices hold for their current and former law clerks.

The magnificent **Library** is also oak paneled, with seven high arches on either side of the room. The woodcarvings include portrayals of famous lawgivers from ancient Greece and Rome, and also include tributes to science, law, art, and other fields of study. The Library holds more than 450,000 books.

To discuss their cases, the justices retreat to their private **Conference Room**. The justices meet there on Wednesdays and Fridays to talk about cases, assign opinions for writing, and review other matters.

How the Court Hears a Case

A typical case at the Supreme Court begins with a petition for a *Writ of Certiorari* from any person or party unhappy with a decision by a lower court. The High Court reviews more than 7,000 petitions a year, some of them handwritten. As the petitions arrive, the justices review them, and they are discussed in private conference. If four of the nine justices feel that a case merits the attention of the court, the court will grant the petition. The lower court then sends a record of the case to the Supreme Court. Typically, the court grants *Certiorari* in only 90 to 100 of the petitions it receives annually. The Supreme Court also has constitutional authority to decide certain other kinds of cases, such as disputes between states. In those cases, the Supreme Court would be the first court to review the case. Whatever the source, the Supreme Court decides only the most important cases, involving the interpretation of the U.S. Constitution.

When the justices agree to hear a case, it is scheduled for oral argument in the Courtroom. Lawyers for each side then file briefs (written arguments) for the justices to read prior to oral arguments. The term

The Tail End

Resources for Parents and Teachers

of the court begins each year on the first Monday in October. Oral arguments are heard October through April, usually for two weeks each month, on Mondays, Tuesdays, and Wednesdays. The Marshal of the Court (the marshal noted here is a court officer, not a justice or a mouse) opens each session with "Oyez! Oyez! Oyez!"—a greeting from the French word for "Hear Ye!" In each case, oral arguments are usually limited to one hour, with lawyers from each side allotted 30 minutes. The justices often ask questions of the lawyers during their presentations to the court.

A case is considered submitted for final decision at the conclusion of the oral argument. The justices again meet in private conference to vote on the cases. (In the illustration of the Conference Room, note that the justices wear normal business attire—not their traditional robes—in these sessions.) It takes a majority of justices to decide a case. If the Chief Justice is in the majority, he will write the opinion himself or assign one of the other justices in the majority to write it. If the Chief Justice is not in the majority, the most senior justice in the majority will write the opinion or assign it. A summary of the opinion is later read out loud in the Courtroom by the justice who wrote it, and the complete opinion is made available in writing to the public the morning it is announced.

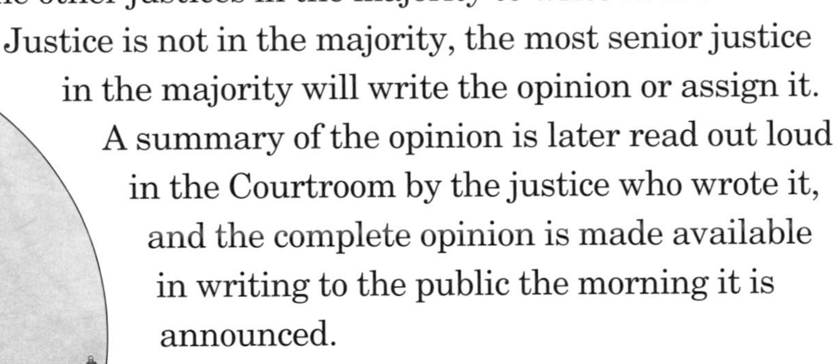

Acknowledgments

The authors wish to acknowledge the invaluable help and support of three members of the Supreme Court staff for their editing and consulting work on this book: Gail Galloway, Catherine E. Fitts, and James C. Duff. We also wish to thank our friends and neighbors, Fred and Amy Upton, for their help and support. And we want to thank the late Kay Ryan, for all the supportive phone calls to Cheryl while she was tied to her drawing desk for many months!

—P.W.B. and C.S.B.